Gone

The Missing Years of Bjorn Esterday

Book 02

AromaX

2030

Wynter Sommers

USA Copyright © 2015 GJ dePillis
© TXu002023789 and TXu002010532 / 2016

Library of Congress Control Number: **2021936597**

Published by Pure Force Enterprises, Inc.
California, USA
Since 2002

INGRAM

INGRAM® Distribution

ISBN13: 978-1-7184-0031-3   ISBN 10: 1-7184-0031-4

DEDICATION

To those who feel strongly about truth, justice, and the integrity of America; your honorable actions make us proud.

To those who wonder if their daily choices matter; your small decisions impact generations to come.

To those everyday people who don't think they have what it takes; your perseverance and strive for the extraordinary, makes the impossible a reality.

To those who have failed; know you will make it and tomorrow will be better.

Your dreams today become our future tomorrow.
Thank you for everything you do.

Bjorn Esterday
Was Not Born Yesterday
Series

Firebrand (15 Volumes+Conversation Station Book)
Edges (9 Stories +Conversation Station Book)
Gone (24 Stories + Conversation Station Book +
Longfellow Journal book for 26 book set)

Bjorn EDGES Series

EDGES Book 1-Swift Encounter
EDGES Book 2-Rousing Attack
EDGES Book 3-One Foot Under
EDGES Book 4-Earthshake
EDGES Book 5-Broken String
EDGES Book 6-Key Witness
EDGES Book 7-Who is She?
EDGES Book 8-Vanish
EDGES Book 9-Chase or Die

Bjorn Series Alternate Reading Plan

ACKNOWLEDGMENTS

We acknowledge those who actively build peace. We acknowledge all the selfless talent which contributed to creating meaningful tokens of consideration and sharing. We acknowledge that every person has a daily choice of right or wrong... and we thank you for choosing the right, good, honorable path filled with integrity because that is the difficult and brave path. Small choices today become lasting monuments of loving hope tomorrow.

CONTENTS

Settings

Locations

- **AromaX**: City of fragrance & fashion

- **Courtly City**: City of solar & other technical products. Bjorn Esterday and Sarah Paradise live here.

- **Brio**: Underwater village

- **Schiermonnikoog** - a tiny island where Longfellow and Warren visit. Originally a West Frisian Island of the Netherlands.

Characters

- **Otto Mattick:** Research assistant at the AromaX lab
- **Doctor Lou Pole Linden:** Works at the AromaX lab
- **Dustin, Austin, Tustin and Justin**, the dogs of Longfellow
- **Warren Piece**: Friend of Longfellow and trainer
- **Longfellow**: Descendant of TallMan (see Firebrand Series) and avid canine enthusiast. Friend of Warren Piece.
-

0

0 PREFACE

Last time we saw Bjorn Esterday, he couldn't shake the identity foisted upon him in Brio prison. Now, it appears he will be a "guest" for an undetermined length of time.

Meanwhile the Daily Memo newspaper as well as the rest of Courtly City continue to live life and don't appear to immediately miss Bjorn. Will anybody realize his present predicament?

Is Courtly City's ally AromaX going through a leadership change? Is that impacting just AromaX citizens or could it seriously impact Courtly City, as well?

1 CHAPTER 04: (2030) AROMAX LAB: LINDEN & MATTICK ONE MONTH EARLIER-NO RESULTS

Otto Mattick, the simple looking, medium height, mousy colored AromaX Research assistant, appeared to be a most forgettable man. He called to his new boss, Doctor Lou Pole Linden, "I have reaped interesting results, but..."

The short, plump Dr. Lou Pole Linden stroked his handlebar mustache, twisting the ends into sharp points. It was something he did when he was forced to concentrate on any boring activity. He would much rather gaze about at his slipshod retrofitted abandoned hospital warehouse, which, although decrepit, was his very own lab given to him by the Twins when they had recently named him Director of Laboratory Research.

Ignoring Otto Mattick's excessively cheerful outburst, Dr. Lou Pole Linden merely muttered to himself as he read his comm.

"The Twins have approved extra money for..." and he trailed off.

Otto Mattick leaned forward, peering over his wireframe glasses to monitor new data from his own latest experiment. The grimy, poorly lit research lab of AromaX city was a hastily retrofitted warehouse of old medical odds-and-ends in an abandoned sector of AromaX City.

This sector didn't use the expensive pink stones from AromaX quarry. Instead, it mimicked the look of dingy pink paints peeling off in strips. Layers of dust and sticky sediment darkened the stone like a shadowy stain which diligent cleansing probably could not remove.

Otto Mattick looked up from his chair. "Why are the Twins giving you extra money?"

Dr. Lou Pole Linden replied, "Did I say the Twins were providing extra funding...out loud?"

"What did the message say?" Otto Mattick persisted. "What is being negotiated with the Twins?"

Dr. Lou Pole Linden snorted, "You are too forgettable to be a leader, Otto Mattick! That is why the Twins deal exclusively with me. Only I negotiate with them. Remember, you can easily be replaced."

Otto Mattick silently noted Dr. Lou Pole Linden's threat.

New shiny equipment, hastily connected to obsolete technology, sat on old dusty tables pushed carelessly against the grimy walls. Scurrying rodents ran around underfoot. Rhythmic beeps of life supported machinery. This all mingled with the faint hiss of respirators, which begged to have a human subject to work on. Instead, the actual test subjects were real collections of trapped rodents held in rusty cages.

"But, I started this research," Otto Mattick protested, "...to help..."

Dr. Linden, who was determined to take all credit...if this project worked, said carefully, "The Twins are willing to give extra funding...if I...I mean we...add on a feature for the project."

"A feature?" Otto replied, "Like a sanitary lab? New equipment?"

Dr. Linden, gloated over the fact that Otto Mattick had once held a position of prestige, but now was forced to be merely a lab assistant. He liked reminding Otto Mattick that he, Dr. Linden, was now in charge.

"No," Dr. Linden remarked, smiling.

"You know you are lucky you work here. I only took you in so you would avoid being executed as a treasonous political prisoner... Result? Because of my generosity, you are alive. In addition, you are not consigned to sleep on the streets. You have a little place of residence, and can support yourself as well as your nephew. I'm your hero. Remember that."

"What do the Twins want, Dr. Linden?" Otto Mattick repeated quietly.

"You Matticks..." Dr. Linden replied shaking his head with mock compassion, "After everything that has happened to your family, I'm surprised you chose to remain in AromaX."

"You know I stay for Topliner's sake," Otto Mattick replied in a humble whisper. "Now, if it pleases you, what did the Twins ask us to do?" Otto Mattick, determined to survive, knew he had to accept any treatment Lou Pole Linden might capriciously mete out.

The self-absorbed Doctor Linden,

slowly turned, unable to resist reaching for one end of his handlebar mustache, then placing his hand in the pocket of his white lab coat.

Then, abruptly, he snapped, "Just tell me the results you've found so far...I can brief you on what the Twins said later," Dr. Linden dismissed.

Otto Mattick inhaled with great patience, "I have been able to increase the life of these artificial fibers and thereby reduce the rejection rate when attached to natural fibers, but..."

"There is that hesitation, again..." Dr. Linden narrowed his eyes in an attempt to discover the truth.

"Dr. Linden," Otto Mattick paused, "I'm afraid our subjects...I'm afraid it won't work... I mean the cost is too great."

"Let me remind you, again," Dr. Linden interrupted, "I am Dr. Lou Pole Linden. I have taken Longfellow's place as chief scientist here. You no longer influence the public of AromaX, and you are now merely my humbled assistant."

"Longfellow would never act like you..." Otto Mattick blurted.

Dr. Linden interrupted Otto.

"I... I... Me... I have been given Longfellow's job. Look around you! Longfellow is no longer in AromaX. Your splendid hero, that great research scientist Longfellow, is long gone. He ran away, terrified of the Twins. He fled. That shows you how powerful the Twins are. Longfellow will never work in any science industry ever again... no matter where he ends up!"

Otto protested, "Longfellow was more than a scientist. He has military training! And is very disciplined."

Dr. Lou Pole Linden spat, "Longfellow is a political agitator who refused to recognize the authority of the Twins. What I am working on would decimate any ragtag peasant army Longfellow may be building."

"Decimate?" Otto asked, "We are working on creating artificial muscles to help those with degenerative muscular disease to ..." Otto Mattick paused and turned to Dr. Lou Pole Linden, "What did the Twins ask you to do?"

Dr. Lou Pole Linden replied, "MagSols...Magnificent Soldiers. The twins want to enhance humans to be the most formidable army around. The note they just sent asked me to add another criterion to the MagSol design." He gave a broad grin. "We will make our MagSols fully functional... under water."

Otto Mattick replied, "Soldiers? So you have abandoned the idea of helping the handicapped?"

Dr. Lou Pole Linden banged his fist on the table and shouted, "We are building MagSols. Magnificent Soldiers! That is what the Twins are paying for. That is where the money is. Do you think it is easy to negotiate with the Twins of

AromaX to keep us fed?" He smiled again and shrugged, "Imagine! All they want in exchange for their money is...results."

"Regardless," Otto Mattick nodded as he had heard that speech many times before, "...we do have an ethical responsibility to conduct safe clinical trials in accordance with regulatory standards... even if we never get audited by any agency. Our goal is to help the handicapped. And I'm finding that if we continue on this path we are now pursuing, the procedure will kill too many subjects."

Dr. Linden twisted the end of his mustache into a fine well-waxed point, then nodded as if he understood. "Your sister is gone, Mr. Mattick. Your artificial muscle fibers cannot help her. You and your nephew are the only Matticks left in AromaX. You need to embrace your loss and move on. I do not want the past to influence your ability to work for me. Embrace your new role as my assistant."

"But..." Otto Mattick started.

Dr. Lou Pole Linden howled in frustration, "We don't have time to go through all this! Your job is now to take your research and build a super strong human soldier who can fight underwater as well as on land. We cannot work with rats anymore. Next, we need a larger subject. A pig! "

Shaking his head, Otto replied, "If it kills a rat, I'm pretty sure we can extrapolate it would be lethal to a pig."

"Then we move on! To a human subject," Dr. Linden reasoned.

Otto's jaw dropped, "You want to take an unproven procedure that has killed all our prior test subjects and try it out on a human? There is no reason to justify..."

Dr. Lou Pole Linden interrupted, "As I was saying before you went on your rant. There is a reason. At this very moment, the Twins are exploring the option of having underwater military facilities.

"Are you listening? Totally underwater. The Twins don't want some scuba diving suit. They want these soldiers to have powers built into them so they will have full functionality underwater. Therefore, we need to produce MagSols, as requested! Pronto!"

"But..."

"The MagSols..." Dr. Lou Pole Linden sniffed, "...that is what the Twins are willing to pay a good deal extra for."

Then Otto Mattick slowly replied, "What about the handicapped? You told me the Twins wanted to alleviate the suffering of the weaker citizens of AromaX."

Dr. Lou Pole Linden shook his head, "No, no, no... that was a campaign slogan. You can't hold the Twins to what they said to get the people of AromaX to support their position as the new rulers."

"I shared my research, which started before the Twins took over to..." Otto

Mattick steadied himself as he slowly turned to face Dr. Lou Pole Linden directly and whispered, "...to help those among us suffering from degenerative muscular diseases. I was executing test cases which would address...

Otto held up his thumb and said, "First, get the artificial muscle fibers to bond to natural fibers..."

Otto held up his pointer finger and continued, "Second, to certify that the skeletal structure is strong enough to support the potential weight, which the new stronger muscles can bear.

"Third, to ensure we stop the degeneration so as not to contaminate any of the freshly implanted muscles..."

"And now," Dr. Linden interrupted Otto, "Now, you only need to use a healthy human subject and make that MagSol operational under water...."

Otto Mattick turned away, shaking his head in disbelief, "Super soldiers?

MagSols?" Otto Mattick scoffed under his breath.

Dr. Lou Pole Linden slowly explained, "The Twins are bent on crippling Courtly City....or any city which seems more powerful than they are. That's how they expand. Besides, don't get all moral on me. If we cannot get the MagSols ready in time, the Twins will contract the AnCors instead and we will be homeless and have to beg the AnCors to take us in."

"MagSols?" Repeated Otto. "I thought you were mocking..."

"Magnificent Soldiers..." Dr. Linden, said with exaggerated patience, "I've been thinking, what else would one call a man who could lift two thousand pounds with one hand? And function under water? Enhanced human? Too boring. I actually like 'MagSol'."

"Boring! How about not in any way a

reality?" Otto shook his head in disbelief, "Besides, you actually think the AnCors would express concern, or even pity on us, if we were in need? They would kill us as soon as look at us. What makes you even dream they'd take us in like kindly Earth Farmers if we were in need?"

"I don't!" Lou Pole Linden barked. "I was being sarcastic. The AnCors work for the Twins. Everybody knows that...don't you?"

Otto Mattick looked over his wire frame glasses and asked, "Then what stops the Twins from giving the AnCors the order to wipe us out?"

Dr. Lou Pole Linden haughtily explained, "The Twins would never turn on me. I've proven myself loyal...unlike the Mattick clan..."

He swiped both ends of his mustache as a dramatic conclusion to his profound statement.

The computer beeped and flashed a notice that their latest experimental efforts had compiled.

"Are those the results of the rat tests?" Dr. Linden asked.

"Yes." Otto reached out to tap some keys and studied the data, grimacing.

Otto Mattick sputtered, "This proves we cannot use humans. The carbon aerogel epoxy polymer composite makes a stronger shield against extreme heat and cold, but we cannot use it for a skeletal structure. The body rejects it. Besides even if it did take, there is a chance it could leak toxins over time, damaging the liver and...."

Dr. Linden shouted, "We also ran a sample set using aggregated diamonds over titanium for a skeletal structure. How did that fare?"

Squinting as he examined the data, Otto replied, "Fullerene nanostructures in hydrogenated amorphous carbon is also strong enough to bear the additional weight of artificial muscle fibers... assuming they were not rejected by the subject. I still maintain that Aerogel, titanium and the Aggregated Diamonds would make a better exoskeleton than an internal skeletal structure exposed to constant bathing in bodily fluids."

Dr. Linden twirled his mustache with a smile.

"Perfect loop hole. If we can't implant the muscle fibers, we can develop something better than a suit of armor that the Twins would assign to an AromaX soldier. We could build an exoskeleton as part of the MagSol's body and that could keep them operational underwater as well as on land."

Otto shook his head, "How did a corporate city like AromaX, known for the finest luxury perfumes, suddenly find an interest in building a formidable army?"

"The Twins' new management direction

or... simple Greed... who knows?" Dr. Linden dismissed Otto Mattick's whispered objection with the wave of his hand, "...It's not my concern. If the Twins are jealous of the organic food production of those Earth Farmers in Courtly City, let them pay us to quell their jealously. Nobody can ever reason with a rich man, let alone the Twins of AromaX. Now....where was I? Oh, yes. Let's build the exoskeleton armor and add on a helmet of Aluminum Oxynitride since it would be three times as strong as steel and that Alumina would be nearly transparent."

"Dr. Lou Pole Linden, transparent does not mean bullet proof..." Otto reminded his new boss.

"So weave in a nano-net of Kevlar," Dr. Lou Pole Linden casually reasoned.

"Abandon the artificial muscle fibers, then? Build a suit of armor?"

"Oh, no. No. No. Those artificial fibers are ten...fifty times stronger than human

18

muscle fiber... Try NanoNevel," Dr. Linden announced.

"That Miasma?" Otto Mattick shook his head and then swiped his hand across a screen to clear away dust and invoke a command to reveal information on the screen. Then he looked up at Dr. Linden. "This lab is not equipped to do nano-surgery."

Dr Linden excitedly peered over Otto Mattick's shoulder, "See? NanoNevel could work."

"But we would need," Otto Mattick sighed, "a coder to develop extensive subroutines to coordinate all those microscopic nano-bots to penetrate the skin and place the musculature in the right place at the right time so that it can still accept nourishment from the host subject. And you still need a conductor of sorts to monitor the process with precision." He turned and looked at Dr. Linden, "and it still could kill the host."

"So, get a coder," Dr. Linden dismissed, "It's this or the streets or the AnCors, my friend," Dr. Linden reminded his destitute research assistant.

"We still don't have a host...not even one of the rats that run around this dump..." Otto retorted, "Let alone a pig."

"Cross breeding humans will take generations," Dr. Lou Pole Linden thought aloud, "Even if we could fuse human DNA with that from a Mimic Octopus."

Otto Mattick replied half entertaining these notions from his supervisor, "I am not suggesting we create a human version of Race de la Moyenne et Haute Belgique..."

Dr. Linden replied, "No. Nobody wants to look like those bulky Belgium Blue cattle even if you do call them by their French name. We need the artificial muscle fibers to attach to a skeletal structure= either of bone or of another substance= and we need that man to appear as if he is of normal size." Linden sighed, "MagSols must be able to infiltrate crowds. If MagSols are too large, they'll be spotted immediately...We should...We need...No... We must have at least one human specimen to immediately begin work on."

"I'm sure a real hospital would have willing volunteers with degenerative..."

Dr. Linden, annoyed, interrupted, "I said no more talk about your sister. No more helping the handicapped. That's it. We are making MagSols, not helping the handicapped. The real money is in war."

"We wouldn't be doing this if the ruling family had stayed together in AromaX..." Otto Mattick murmured.

Dr. Lou Pole Linden placed fists akimbo on his hips and said, "Look. Accept life as it is. The Twins were bullies and nobody thought they would take over, but they did. So now we live in their world and by their rules. Hey, I'd like to live under Jack Courtly's rule in

Courtly City, also, but we'd still need the Twins, in their position as the new AromaX leadership, to grant us approval to live in Courtly City."

"And the Twins won't do that because they want us to finish this job...."

Otto Mattick nodded reluctantly understanding his predicament.

Dr. Linden paused for a moment, motionless while he thought, then said, "But, we can visit Courtly City as tourists and I happen to know Watson is about to host his convention at the Courtly City Convention Center. He always has good ideas. Maybe he can get me a Mimic Octopus...anyway. I might be able to arrange it with Watson's assistant, Tres."

"You would ask Watson...a motivational speaker...a...a...performer... about scientific matters? About adding on the capability for a soldier to operate fully underwater?" Otto Mattick asked aghast. He shook his head, "I'm glad

Topliner isn't working here."

Dr. Linden retorted, "Your nephew, Topliner, is an over privileged brat. Adds no value. Anywhere...Watson has culled devoted clientele from all the corporations. AromaX and Courtly City, included. You might even know some devoted disciples of Watson's...like your sister, Topliner's mother... Besides, Watson knows people. He'll help us if there is something for him to gain by it," Dr. Linden sneered, then added, "You know, Otto, you are not adding value right now, either. Why don't you just go home and ponder how you could add value tomorrow."

Otto Mattick, hurried home through the littered neglected streets of AromaX to his tiny cluttered living quarters. He remembered how he used to insist on pristine public areas, but now ...he was helpless to influence anything. He dwelled on his present task at hand. He had to speak urgently with his nephew, Topliner.

2 CHAPTER 05: (2030) AROMAX APARTMENT: OTTO MATTICK THAT EVENING SPEAKS WITH TOPLINER

"Did you read the news?" Topliner called to his Uncle as Otto Mattick hurried through the door of their tiny flat.

The place was crowded with old balloon furniture. The walls, carelessly painted a dull pink, were an attempt to imitate the color theme of AromaX natural stones, which were used in constructing the luxury buildings over on the other side of town.

Since Otto had to get used to his new demeaned status, he no longer lived in pampered luxury. Instead, he was forced to acclimate to his current, decrepit accommodations, which he now had to share with his nephew, Topliner.

Topliner sat on the floor unfolding a deflated plastic chair, and then started to exhale into the mouthpiece to fill it up.

Otto Mattick closed and locked the flimsy door which was painted a brass color, because this building could not afford genuine brass.

"What news?" Otto asked exhausted and a little annoyed at his nephew. "You mean the news that you paid off your debts?" Otto shook his head, "When I think about how we have fallen...the luxuries we used to..."

"I mean the news in Courtly City, Uncle Otto," Topliner emphasized and resumed blowing into the mouthpiece.

Otto took two strides to a shelf, got the bicycle air pump, and handed it to Topliner to use to inflate the balloon chair. Topliner took it silently and started pumping.

"I don't care about Courtly City. I care that we live in this hole because you squandered the money from your mother. The only pay I get from the lab is this apartment, a box of deflated furniture, and food. If you don't watch yourself, Topliner, they'll come for you. Hurt you...hurt me." Otto shook his head.

Then Otto Mattick flopped down onto an already inflated cassock, which started to whistle as the air squealed out of it. Topliner tossed Otto a roll of tape to block the hole, but Otto lacked the scissors to cut a strip of tape off from the roll, so left the roll hanging from the cubed cassock after the hole was patched. The cassock was now partially deflated.

With a smirk, Topliner smugly replied, "You'd never let anything happen to me because I'm all that's left of...her..."

"Just tell me your news," Otto snapped impatient with his nephew.

Slowly Topliner looked his Uncle Otto in the eye and said, "An old copy of a Courtly City Newspaper said that Jack and Queenie Courtly...everybody aboard... are dead. Train accident. Maybe it will be easier for us Matticks to relocate, now...Fresh start! Uncle Otto. Imagine. Fresh start!"

Otto paused for a moment before replying, "Was it a real accident or were the AnCors involved?"

Otto pushed himself up awkwardly from his partially deflated seat as the chair Topliner was pumping up, was now fully inflated. He shoved the balloon chair toward his Uncle Otto. It bounced a couple of times before Otto grabbed and steadied the chair and eased himself down.

Otto was stunned, "Wait a minute? Jack and Queenie Courtly are both dead? Train accident? Are you sure..."

Topliner shrugged, "I dunno. I'm not like that friend of yours, Warren Piece. What ever happened to him, anyway? It's been a while since you mentioned him or Longfellow."

Otto shook his head, "Warren Piece and Longfellow left AromaX some time ago. Last I heard, Longfellow got a service job with some foreign family."

"But," his nephew persisted, "Didn't you say Longfellow was planning a wedding and was worried he'd lose his job? Kind of sad for a smart guy like him to be worried about losing a servant job when he once was a respected scientist."

Topliner shuffled on his knees over to the cassock his uncle had occupied earlier and took scissors to snip off the roll of tape, which Otto had just used to plug the hole. Topliner sat on the cassock and leaned over with the sharp scissors to cut off the tape.

As Otto stood up, Topliner accidentally jabbed the inflated cassock with the scissors popping it with a loud bang.

Otto ignored what just happened and calmly said, "We all have to make sacrifices these days. Longfellow and Warren will stick together, but I have no idea where they are. I just remember Longfellow's last communication with me was before you and I moved into this shoe box... and before the Twins set up the barrier, which blocked our communications."

Topliner asked, "So, last you heard, was Longfellow coming back to AromaX?"

Topliner took the exploded cassock and tossed it into the corner with other already torn and exploded plastic balloon furniture. He opened a small box and pulled out another folded plastic unit. He used the bicycle pump to fill it up. They never knew what shape might inflate until the air would give it form. This one looked as if it would be a coffee table with four fat legs.

Otto rubbed his eyes.

"I don't think Longfellow will come back to AromaX. I just don't know. What I do know is that Lou Pole Linden wants to plan a trip to Courtly City."

"Why do you say it like that?" Topliner asked as, panting, he vigorously pumped up the plastic coffee table.

Otto sneered sarcastically.

"Maybe I don't trust my new boss, Dr. Lou Pole Linden, because of the way he got Longfellow's position."

"I don't blame you. I don't like him, either," Topliner smiled a huge grin. "So, can I have a party when you go off to Courtly City?"

He sat in the middle of the now inflated coffee table and it sank under his weight until Topliner was essentially sitting on the floor.

Otto glared at his nephew, "No, Topliner. As a matter of fact, you're coming with me."

3 CHAPTER 06: (2030) ISLAND LONGFELLOW: THE ISLAND RECRUITS STAND UP TO MEET LONGFELLOW

Longfellow, former Chief Scientist of the AromaX science and labs division, clenched his fists as he looked out over the grey waters of the Wadden Sea. The sand was cold under his bare feet. The forested island stretched out behind him.

He gritted his teeth as he recalled how he had been displaced from his fragrance-research directorship of

AromaX city by the cunning tricks of Dr. Lou Pole Linden. It seemed so long ago.

Dr. Lou Pole Linden was probably twisting his handlebar mustache as he ordered the lab staff to focus on some shoddy shortcut with promises of riches if they provided instant results.

Longfellow was only on this island to achieve specific goals. Things would be made right when he got back to AromaX, and he was once again calling the shots.

After a long moment, Longfellow turned to whistle, then shouted, "Justin! Austin! Dustin! Here! Now!" Waves of the Wadden Sea softly lapped along the beach of the small island, one of many tiny islands in this Necklace of the Netherlands district.

In response, only one dog raced to Longfellow. He smiled when the dog, Justin, arrived and sat panting at his feet.

Longfellow, formerly of AromaX, often went to the shore to exercise his dogs and gaze out onto the rippling salty grey waters.

Now that Longfellow had left his service job with the family in Utrecht, Longfellow frequently pondered if he had chosen correctly. Was this the path in life he should take?

Longfellow wondered how Otto Mattick and his nephew Topliner were doing in AromaX. Otto had told Longfellow he himself had to stay in AromaX...for Topliner's sake. Otto owed it to his own sister even though she was gone. Then the Twins had set up their barrier and all communication was halted. Now Longfellow only had memories.

Longfellow frequently thought of the people he respected back in AromaX. He felt the pain of anguish as he recalled those cherished friends who, he hoped, had escaped when the Twins took over... and the sad lives of those who had decided to stay.

He inhaled cool salty mist and exhaled slowly. Longfellow was glad Warren Piece had found him.

After Longfellow fled from AromaX, he urgently needed some place to stay. An old friend of the former ruling family of AromaX had offered Longfellow a position on their domestic staff. Longfellow swallowed his pride with pragmatic determination and took the job. He was no longer a scientist, no longer the highly respected Director of Research in the laboratories of AromaX. Now he was a servant... obedient... submissive...

But Longfellow realized he had to reinvent himself and blend into the background until the Twins would forget all about him and stop hunting.

They did.

Warren Piece had come bearing that good news right after a family wedding made Longfellow's service position redundant.

When it was deemed safe, Longfellow left domestic service and the family in Utrecht. As a parting gift, they had loaned Longfellow a large house near the islands and a winery to tend some distance away in Maastricht not far from the golden labyrinth of caves.

Both the house and winery were in remote locations. The family said it was only until Longfellow would be able to get back on his feet.

Warren Piece helped him run the winery so they could collect enough money to fund their return to AromaX.

This family in Utrecht had been unexpectedly kind and generous because of what had happened to their own family and friends when the Twins took over.

Longfellow squinted into the sun, then felt the furry warmth of another dog by his legs. He looked down.

Justin, the Belgium Malinois, had been given to Longfellow as a gift, back when he was still in domestic service for the Utrecht family. A retired Soldier-Police officer from Courtly City had been a guest of the man who employed Longfellow.

When this retired ex-SP, ex-Soldier-Police, had visited the Utrecht family, he invited his son, an active Courtly City SP, to join him.

Since most corporations designed their own cities these days, there was an immediate need to develop a force of authority. Such authorities combined the law-keeping mandates of the police of yesteryear, along with the military training of soldiers of tomorrow. Therefore, the soldier-police were commonly referred to as SPs.

Longfellow absently petted the dogs which looked up at him expectantly, waiting for his next command.

Sandy grass-tufted beach spread out around him. He closed his eyes and listened to the soft lapping of gentle waves. Longfellow's location was quietly conveyed by Warren Piece to other AromaX refugees. Piece encouraged them to join Longfellow, here in this place.

Strength in numbers, Warren would say. In addition, the Utrecht estate entrusted to Longfellow, was large enough to accommodate the growing number of recruits.

Longfellow called out again. "Dustin, Austin. Come!" Then, two more dogs ran toward him.

Dustin, the black Labrador Retriever, was an excellent companion when hunting water fowl.

Austin, the brave little Jack Russel Terrier could track anything on land.

Longfellow gazed out toward the ocean and along the shores of the islands nestled in the Wadden Sea.

"Good workout," Longfellow said to his pack of dogs, "but she's not coming today, so we may as well go home."

Sometimes Longfellow would recall the woman he had loved back in AromaX. Her name was Pris. He would fantasize that Pris might arrive on the shores of this beach like Botticelli's painting, the "Birth of Venus". He envisioned a huge oyster shell opening and his pearl, his love, emerging, reaching for his hand... He knew it was unrealistic, but thinking of her made him smile.

Longfellow noted that a few yards away, Tustin, the poodle, was being groomed by his old friend, Warren Piece.

Ah, Warren Piece. He would always set Longfellow straight, and remind Longfellow that the true love Longfellow remembered, and waited for, was truly gone. Period. Gone.

Warren was sympathetic to Longfellow's preoccupation, but believed it was important to frequently remind him to face facts. Warren Piece knew both of them. Warren Piece would remind Longfellow to sober up from the soft feathery touch of Pris' intoxicating memories. Warren Piece was a realist. They had more than the winery to manage. They created their headquarters in this place. They had to keep focused.

Longfellow sighed.

With the dogs and Warren Piece, his old friend from AromaX, this was all the family Longfellow really needed. At least that is what he told himself just to stop himself from dwelling on hopeless fantasies of finding her.

Working at the winery was not like working with AromaX flowers, developing botanicals and blending fragrances as he had done before escaping when the Twins took over. Clearly, however, working in this Maastricht winery was still dealing with plants, but now he was producing wine instead of fragrance. It was his present life.

The dogs excitedly wagged their tails as they panted after that hard daily workout.

Turning his back to the water, Longfellow broke into a steady run.

The dogs, including, Austin, the Jack Russel Terrier jogged behind him. Then, Justin, the Belgian Malinois barked.

Longfellow stopped.

The dogs looked up at Longfellow, curious and then their attention locked onto the approaching man.

"You were down at the beach, again?" Warren Piece asked as he held the leash of a white poodle named Tustin.

"I needed to work them out," Longfellow explained indicating his dogs.

"Well, I finished grooming Tustin, here," Warren Piece replied as he handed the leash to Longfellow. "Our recruits have been waiting for over an hour back at headquarters...."

Longfellow took the leash, and started walking with his poodle Tustin and his three off-leash dogs, Austin, Dustin, and Justin. "Let's go."

After several minutes, Longfellow paused, then pointed to Dustin and Austin and commanded, "Elegant".

Both dogs raced off. Tustin remained on the leash and Justin stayed by Longfellow's side.

"Longfellow, the recruits are still waiting at the house, waiting for you to train them," Warren Piece impatiently leaned in closer as they waited. "Look. She's gone. You have a new life. Nobody here knows who you were. You don't need to go gazing out at the ocean every day. Pris is not coming in on some tide and we need to put together an army. You're the leader. You've got to keep your head focused for the sake of the recruits!"

Dustin and Austin returned, each with a package in his mouth. Longfellow reached down and took one bag from Austin and Warren Piece took the bag from Dustin. Inside were small bow ties.

Warren Piece commented, "I still can't believe that you felt fetching their own doggie bow ties was such a useful task that you trained them with that word," Warren Piece muttered. "Elegant."

Longfellow commented as they resumed walking, "If we are to take AromaX back from the Twins, we need a long-term strategy, not just an army. They have more resources and will always outgun us. But, on the other hand, we could outsmart them. Showing the recruits how well the dogs are trained, means they will also learn refinements to socially engineer a take-over. By now, I think we both realize we will never have the resources for a confrontational military attack."

Longfellow paused and then knelt down as he affixed a bow tie to Justin's collar and then Austin's collar.

While managing to position Dustin's bow tie onto his collar, Longfellow noticed Warren struggling with the fidgety cloud-white poodle, Tustin.

Warren sighed as he attempted to attach the bow tie onto Tustin's collar. Warren shook his head as he realized this process was taking more time than expected. Smiling, Longfellow reached for the bow tie as Warren impatiently slapped it into Longfellow's hand. Effortlessly, Longfellow took the bow tie and deftly secured it onto Tustin's collar. The white poodle sat there wagging his well-groomed tail looking up at Warren, then back at Longfellow as if the dog were watching a tennis match.

"And now these islands are my home," Longfellow sighed as he stood up.

"No," Warren corrected, "These islands are your training grounds where you will stay and recharge until you refine a plan to take back AromaX."

Warren led the way up the path, but suddenly stopped and beckoned Longfellow to follow him. Earlier, when he couldn't find Longfellow, Warren Piece had placed the basket containing a bottle of wine and glasses on the ground. Now he collected the basket, uncorked the bottle and poured a glass, handing it to Longfellow.

"Taste," Warren Piece prompted. Longfellow accepted the glass and took a sip.

"Mr. Piece," Longfellow started, "I do declare," he laughed, "that this front of a business, here at the Maastricht winery, is actually producing a very fine vintage, indeed."

Warren Piece gave a brief nod and spoke with a smile, "Glad you approve this sampling of the vintage I brought from the winery." Warren then asked, "So, is it your plan to teach the recruits to balance grit with refinement? Is that why you are asking the dogs to wear bow ties?"

Longfellow replied, "To prove my strategy of social engineering, I want to introduce the pack as docile dogs. Then, the recruits will see them in action. Our recruits, too, must learn to be gracious, and only become dangerous when absolutely needed. They will learn discipline...not just simple minded brute force. I've noticed our recruits are quick to instigate fights amongst each other, as if that is an effective way to defend our AromaX honor. Realistically, however, we need to teach them to conquer an enemy with cunning, along with integrity."

Warren replied, "Nothing wrong with a targeted attack."

"Warren," Longfellow frowned, "...we can reinforce the wisdom that difficult situations we encounter must first be navigated with diplomacy... and manners. The act of killing is a last resort. It should surprise the enemy. Strength of character is as important as strength in body. Brute force is worthless without the ability to make the right choice in the split second of a hot battle. Now, what plan of..."

Warren interrupted him with a sweeping gesture.

"What are you so worried about? The Twins can't bother us in these islands, this 'necklace of the Netherlands'. Here we can train the recruits unimpeded."

Longfellow twisted his mouth as he glanced at the watery horizon. "It's only a few islands. Isn't it more like the choker of the Netherlands? Maybe a bracelet?"

"I think you are missing the point, Longfellow," Warren Piece admonished. "There are more islands than these right there off the shores."

Longfellow nodded with a grin, "You are right. The Twins are busy deciding on their next conquest," Longfellow agreed. "They've forgotten about me, so we can train here."

"Workout in the morning, then refinement at night?" Warren Piece asked.

"The Texel Dunes are perfect for a workout. The sand will provide resistance to challenge their muscles as they run. Then our recruits can commune with the seals of Ecomare."

"You are focusing only on agility?" Warren asked, as they walked along the cobblestones of the village toward the main house.

"No," Longfellow replied as he opened the door to the house and walked in. "Each island replicates a small version of an area in AromaX. Sand dunes, forest, swamplands... In each segment we work to develop specific military tactics along with physical strengths..." Longfellow continued, "When they achieve the designated action goals, we hike or swim back. Then I collect the culinary specialties of each place after the morning workout. When recruits arrive back here, they are instructed how to behave in non-combat venues with usefully appropriate manners."

"Culinary specialties?" Warren asked

as they prepared to make themselves comfortable before the blazing fireplace.

Longfellow, still holding his wineglass, used a hand command and all of his dogs, Dustin, Austin, Tustin, and Justin lay down at his feet, as Longfellow situated himself in an overstuffed leather chair.

He took a sip of wine and continued to explain to Warren Piece, "After our recruits learn to navigate through the forests of Vlieland, and get to the red lighthouse, they can replenish their strength with one of the nutritious cranberry dishes made in the village."

Warren asked, "Where will you teach them how to fight in swampland?"

Longfellow smiled, "At the marshes in Terschelling".

Surprised, Warren asked, "Wait. That's where the first tower was built in

1323 and the Brandaris lighthouse...that was built in 1594? What's the point? These recruits know nothing of history, particularly that Brandaris is the oldest lighthouse around. That's the culture of the Netherlands. Not AromaX."

"But," Longfellow said, "...their training should include history. Understanding the history of other lands, as well as their own lineage, will help them make appropriate choices in our present day. They need to know more than where to place a kick or aim a weapon.

Warren retorted, "Wait, these are former AromaX residents fleeing from the oppression of the Twins just like we did. They are not professional military."

Longfellow frowned, "But they also need to understand why they are doing what we are guiding them to do. They need to align their character to the highest standard. And, remember, they need to be comfortably conversant with the elite classes."

"And when will you teach them how to train animals, as you have?" Warren asked.

Longfellow replied, "I will teach them the basics, but the recruits cannot be paired with a dog until each recruit proves to be loyal, responsible, disciplined, and noble of character."

"You're sure?" warned Warren. "I don't think they would know how to even catch a fish, if they needed to."

Longfellow nodded, "They also need to master fishing and equestrian skills. I think Nes Ameland would be the best place for that."

Warren smiled, "Oh, they will enjoy the Ameland catfish on rye bread with a touch of mustard. And after a workout, you should go to each village and bring back the special cheese they make on that island to pair with our wines."

Ignoring Warren's sarcasm, Longfellow advised, "It would be better if we planned a trip to Alkmaar and explore the cheese market."

"But do they have Schiermonnikoog honey for our tea?" Warren grinned.

"You only like Schiermonnikoog because it is the tiniest island of all." Longfellow chortled, "We simply need to use what is around us to discipline these recruits."

"Strong in body, strong in mind, and refined in culture," Warren parroted.

"Well," Longfellow shrugged, "If we can train them to behave in public as if manners were second nature, then they will be polished and genteel, yet deadly enough to penetrate the forces of the Twins."

"When will you know they are ready?" Warren asked.

"I can't state a date or place," Longfellow shook his head. "I'll observe how they behave in the gardens of

Keukenhof before we venture to another country to get supplies. They need to remember to bring flowers, an odd number and never thirteen, as a gift when invited over for dinner. They need to learn so much."

"I'll tell you what we need. We need to make new alliances to get AromaX back," Warren suggested.

Longfellow smiled, "My family has already established alliances."

Warren Piece shook his head, "Oh, Longfellow, not that again. You can't even find his descendants with the hope you can call in a favor."

Longfellow leaned forward and set his glass down, "My family roots demand that I and my offspring honor a multi-generational agreement. I am sure whoever he, or she, is will do the same and honor their forefather's promises."

"You mean," Warren clarified, "because your great, great, great ancestor made a promise with someone back in the 1770's, you would seek out that man's descendant to ask for help?"

Longfellow looked at him, "My ancestor TallMan received a promise, and I will be the generation to collect. I am honor bound by my ancestor's word."

Warren asked, "Then why don't you call on one of his descendants today to get you back to AromaX?"

"Because," Longfellow replied, "I've never met any of them."

Warren thought aloud as he stood up and walked toward large closed doors across the way, "If ever there was a time to call in a favor, now would be it. How would you recognize one of these descendants?"

"I smuggled out the box when I escaped from AromaX..." Longfellow recalled.

"But," Warren asked, "How can a diary

and an old scrap of blue silk fabric, bits of cork and some ancient document about liberty or something which the corporate cities don't even abide by... I mean how can any of that junk connect you to one of TallMan's friends' descendants?"

Longfellow got up and beckoned his dogs to follow him, "They were more than friends. TallMan and his mother's interventions saved the life of Button Gwinette's offspring. Out of gratitude, Button promised his offspring would always be honor-bound to be allied with TallMan's descendants...and that box proves I am a descendant of TallMan. Trust me, when I meet him or her, that generational alliance will be honored."

"Fine," said Warren. "You are Tallman's descendant. Do you even have a name for the friend of Tallman who will reveal this descendant? Who will come forward to help you? Now?"

"Yes. One. Button Gwinette."

"Oh. And his present day descendant is... where?" Warren asked, "And what if his family wasn't as good about history as you are? What if he or she doesn't even know about this promise from the 1770's? Or, if they do, what if they are not in a position to honor it...or simply won't?"

After a long pause, Longfellow quietly replied, ."I don't know..."

Warren explained, "Look, The Twins took what was not theirs. The takeover scattered and killed AromaX citizens. Even your trusted assistant betrayed you..."

Longfellow shook his head, "Please. No mention of Dr. Lou Pole Linden. He was always out for fame and fortune. I was foolish to have trusted him to remain loyal, and I was played for a fool."

Warren consoled, "Don't berate yourself for a deal Lou Pole Linden made with the Twins. The Twins are ruthless. After you escaped, he might have offended them and now he, himself, could be on the run. We don't know the consequences of Lou Pole Linden's poor choices."

Warren Piece took a deep breath and and gave Longfellow a friendly slap on the shoulder. "Listen, I know the takeover ripped your lab apart and scattered everyone loyal to the old order. But family is simply whoever decides to care for your well-being. Family is a unit designed to protect you and help you be the best you can be... A team you can count on and who counts on you... And with that definition of family..."

"With your definition of family..." Longfellow smiled as he shook his head, "That means you, Warren Piece, and Tustin, Justin, Dustin, and Austin are my family, now."

"And the recruits..." Warren added.

Longfellow commented, "You realize training the recruits to be both refined and ferocious is only the first hurdle.

Then we must try to find a way to penetrate barriers."

"And take back the AromaX Boardroom?" Warren asked.

"Or die trying..." muttered Longfellow.

After a long silent moment, Longfellow added, "You know... Revenge won't bring my loved ones back...Maybe we should simply earn money from the Maastricht wines, train the recruits to work in the vineyards... and accept that this is our new life..."

Warren Piece stopped and stared at Longfellow. "Would you allow such a grave injustice to go unpunished? Aren't you the one who said Proverbs 17:15 to verse 18 states that acquitting the guilty is just as bad as condemning the innocent? You and I and hundreds of others were innocent. We were condemned unjustly and the wicked, the Twins, yes! The Twins! Were never punished and their evil has spread... it could spread even to the good and innocent people of these remote islands. Don't you have a duty as a leader to at least try to secure Justice?"

Warren halted and faced Longfellow.

"It's not merely for you...it's for all the AromaX refugees scattered everywhere. I know we can't get the Courtly City Daily Memo newspaper out here, but if you remember, before the Twins set up that barrier, we had access to the truth about what was happening."

"I remember," Longfellow replied softly. "I was the one who negotiated with Jack Courtly about leasing fields for AromaX flowers. The Daily Memo covered the story."

Warren replied, "Ah! The Daily Memo. Solid news."

Longfellow nodded, "It's the only source of news where you can trust journalistic research. Since they print on paper, you have a permanent record of the facts. They even store past issues at

Library."

Warren agreed, "It does seem to always have well researched articles."

Longfellow added, "Scribe. Sammy Scribe is the editor. He runs the Daily Memo. I met him, you know."

Warren asked, "Good guy?"

Longfellow spoke quietly, "Sammy Scribe said the field leasing was a great story. Showed the alliance between all Earth Farmers of Courtly City and AromaX. He said that I was instrumental in convincing the Courtly Family to allow anybody from AromaX to do a fast-track relocation to Courtly City. No hassles."

"Yeah," Warren replied, "But with the Twins' barrier, it's not so easy for a refugee to find a place to live these days. And somehow the refugees are finding you, Longfellow. They're looking to you. To lead them."

Longfellow remained silent and looked

down at his well-trained dogs, who silently stared back up at him.

"Longfellow, listen," Warren said with a solemn expression, "The Twins capturing AromaX hurt a lot of people. Please consider these... well... kids... these recruits... who found you here."

Longfellow drew a breath as if about to speak, then allowed Warren to continue.

Warren added with a knowing look, "Your recruits need a strong leader. You have to be that rock-solid father figure, now. Tell you what. Fantasize about a future headline in the Daily Memo. The barrier is down and you have helped a remnant of AromaX survive. A top reporter interviews you. Sammy Scribe would slap you on the back and tell you what a great story it was...."

Longfellow looked away from Warren Piece. After a long moment, he clicked his tongue and called, "Come on Dustin, Austin, Tustin and Justin. Time to meet the new recruits, our extended family of

AromaX refugees."

Inside the large house, at the sound of the door opening, the waiting recruits stood up with respectful military discipline.

4 CHAPTER 07: (2030) COURTLY CITY: SARAH CONDO: SARAH AND GEORGIA HEAD TO TRAIN STATION TO GO OUT

Sarah Paradise, exhausted school teacher, couldn't wait to get back through the front door of her building. Inside, she smiled as her Courtly City running shoes squeaked along the worn black granite floors. She greeted the doorman with a tired smile, trying to hide the stress of her day.

"Today's Daily Memo, Miss Paradise." The door man smiled and handed her a newspaper from the stack he had at his desk.

"Thank you," Sarah replied as she tucked it under her arm, then hurried up the stairs and down the hall to get to the door of her condo.

Sarah held her purse up to her door and the lock clicked open. She quickly slipped into her condo and shut the door behind her, resting her full body weight against it, now safe in the sanctuary of her own place.

Here, she had taken deliberate effort to combat the stark black, steel and crystal, of many Courtly City buildings by decorating her place with bright white walls accented with cheery colors, which reminded her of a sunrise bursting over a verdant grassy knoll.

Sarah often visited Library, where she would find paper-paged books filled with pictures of serene azure blue skies, and pastel baroque chapels accented in glinting gold, brilliant jewel-toned fruits, and an array of subtle tints found in the feathers of birds and the fur of soft cuddly animals. She used colors from all the images she could recollect to create a mental sanctuary which made a happy contrast to the world in which she was employed to work every day.

Sarah sighed. She had made it here. To her refuge. Her very own place where she felt safe. Home.

She was going to relax, go to bed, and then start it all again tomorrow morning in that dingy concrete worn-out school.

The school looked the way Sarah felt at the end of each day, desperately in need of some consideration, filled with hope, yet neglected by those who would benefit most by caring for it.

She shook her head. Division Administrators always had plenty of money for themselves, but none for classrooms, nor student supplies, nor teachers, like Sarah.

Several weeks earlier, Sarah Paradise had planned to take her young class on a field trip to Library.

On her way to meet them, an ACA, Anti Corporate Activity alert, was announced. All wheeled vehicles were, by law, immediately halted and forbidden to operate in Courtly City during such alerts.

Sarah was often made late because of a sudden ACA. Everybody was delayed; it was part of life.

Sarah sometimes reviewed old books on politics in Library. Leadership which allowed corruption to sneak into the ranks of decision makers often led to a slow decay of services available to the general public. Trust, safety, planning for tomorrow eroded with bad leaders.

What was a poor boss? One who would only surround themselves with people who were loyal to them and not to consistent objective truth and ethics. A bad leader kept changing the goals so that staff could never meet those goals. The purpose was to frustrate and discourage so that staff would not have the energy to look into the bad things that bad leader was doing. Bad leaders refuse to be accountable for their actions. They believe if they speak it, it is true. They enjoy people fighting and sabotaging each other to get into the fleeting temporary good graces of that bad boss who attained power with lies, force, and persistent greed for power.

The Twins were an example, but Sarah could never mention them in the classroom. Twins gained power - one corporate city at a time- with ruthless force. They promoted agreeable men to decision making positions, not capable men...just loyal ones. This ensured the Twins remained in power. It ensured the uncertainty of the public so they would worry about something and never have the energy to check and see if what they were fighting was even happening or if it was propaganda, an illusion, which was promoted to distract the public from genuine issues. The Twins promoted officials tasked with disrupting, obstructing progress, and ensuring disruption.

Mrs. Libris once told her an Earth Farmer shared Matthew chapter twelve, verse 22 to 28. Mrs. Libris explained to Sarah that a house divided falls... this is what the Twins needed before they took over a corporate city. Mrs. Libris was the only person Sarah felt safe talking to about such matters.

Sarah sighed. At least she lived in a city where the Courtly family reigned. She may not be a fan of Skipper Courtly, the current corporate presidential leader, but at least he was not the Twins.

Sarah recalled that day she had been delayed by an ACA. Her plans to take the train were interrupted. How did she meet her awaiting class at Library?

She smiled.

What had happened to that , kind and considerate reporter from the Daily Memo? The reporter, who galloped her from a crowded train station locked down from an ACA to Library on his Daily Memo issued steed. He was named Bjorn Esterday. He was a sharp fellow. He wasn't born yesterday.

After Bjorn dropped her off and galloped away; and after Mrs. Libris started to explain why Library was important, Sarah learned something new.

To her dismay, Sarah had been informed by a messenger from her school about a recently authorized regulation. She had just been informed that exposing children to unauthorized non-Administrator-approved material, like all the contents on the book-shelves of Library, was now a punishable teaching offense.

The consequences of exposing her entire class to the multiple resources at Library had resulted in disciplinary action for Sarah.

As a result of that field trip, Sarah's punishment had been an abrupt mid-term transfer from teaching at elementary school to getting placed at a High School assignment across town. Her comm was removed. She became digitally isolated. Her credits were cut so she had to be very careful with her budget.

Sarah sighed.

She had explained to that admirable helpful and considerate Bjorn Esterday where she worked...at the elementary school... not her new sudden assignment across town at the high school.

Shrugging, Sarah reasoned Bjorn never contacted her. He was an investigative reporter. He could have found her if he wanted to make the effort. He probably was not interested in continuing a friendship with a teacher. That would be cross-professions, which was discouraged in Courtly City. Stay with your own kind. He sort of galloped away on his horse that day and ....vanished...gone.

The seemingly capricious administrator-directed punishment for Sarah, did teach her to keep a low profile.

It was not Library the Administration was afraid of; it was teaching an entire classroom to research objective facts and come to a conclusion with an evidence-based logically-assembled conclusion.

"Critical thinking" is what it had been called in one of the paper-page books Sarah read. It was a skill Sarah had and she wanted to share it.

It did not matter that the trip to Library had been initially approved by management, by the student's parents, and the librarian, Mrs, Libris. Administration transferred her to High School students, Sarah learned later, because they would not listen to teachers and so could not be taught the skill of critical thinking... or so Administration thought.

Sarah had been consumed with all these recent changes in her life that this was the first time she had thought about that day with Bjorn Esterday.

Why was Sarah still thinking about him? Should she look him up at the Daily Memo? Maybe it was better to remain disheartened by Bjorn's apparent indifference.

She thought a moment. She definitely did not feel brave enough to march down to his place of business just to say, "Hello…"

Sarah walked to her small dining table and picked up an old copy of the Daily Memo. She placed the copy she had just received next to it. She shook her head.

Each day, Sarah had to devise new lesson plans for her High School students. All those plans were exclusively drawn from approved learning material. She also had to deal with the clearly hostile attitude so evident in these older students.

Each day exhausted her.

"I don't have the energy to look anybody up," Sarah murmured as she sank into her soft couch realizing she was not brave, nor bold...she was just accepting of her current life situation.

She reached across to the table where she had just placed the Daily Memo and turned the pages to scan for Bjorn Esterday's name.

Nothing.

She shook her head. He had not authored any articles in this edition, either. He had just disappeared from their pages. She set it aside. Her eyes closed as she sank into the throw pillows on her sofa. Maybe he got into trouble for giving her a ride to Library. Maybe she should simply stop thinking about him.

He was gone.

As soon as she exhaled with sleepy contentment, there was a knock on her door.

Sarah Paradise, Courtly City High School teacher, heaved herself up from the comfortable sofa inside her peaceful condo-sanctuary and went to greet her visitor, whoever that might be.

When Sarah opened her door, Georgia Peach, a math teacher at Sarah's new school, walked in without an invitation.

"Honey," Georgia drawled, "Simply because you have just arrived at our school does not mean you get to rest after school lets out."

Sarah wore her long hair in a simple ponytail or bun most days, but Georgia always had a well-sculpted coiffure, which reminded Sarah of old fashioned glamour stars from yesteryear. Georgia wore enough makeup to be ready for her photo-shoot at a moment's notice. Georgia was never without a compact mirror to make sure her makeup was flawless throughout the day. Sarah, on the other hand, would clean up in the morning, and not look at herself again until it was time to wash up for bed.

Sarah welcomed her co-worker in and closed the door behind Georgia, "I was just going to make a quiet dinner and work on lessons for classes tomorrow. Do you realize the amount of paperwork the Administrators are having me do, Georgia?"

Sarah walked into her little kitchen. She pulled a chicken from her freezer and slipped the iced bird into the kitchen sink with a thud.

"Sugar, you have got to get out and flirt!" Georgia announced as she flopped onto the sofa and patted a spot near her to indicate Sarah should sit down. "I mean you can't give your number out if you don't have a comm, Sugar, now can you?" She snapped her fingers, "You know there is a convention in town. I'll bet it's winding down right about now. You know what that means..."

Sarah groaned, "Georgia, I do not want to go to some Watson convention. I'm already sick of all the marketing for that thing. I couldn't bear to actually go there.

Even a famous motivational speaker like Watson can't motivate me to go, Georgia."

Georgia shook her dyed red locks and said, "Sugar, Sweetie pie, we are not going to attend the Watson convention. We are going there to see what men are attending the convention and merely strike up a conversation."

"You come over here on a school night? And really want to go out?" Sarah asked amazed, still standing. "I say no to man hunting at a self-help cultie convention. No thank you. Why didn't you say something at school about plans to go out tonight?"

Georgia pouted, "I only came up with the idea when I saw a little old message on my comm about the convention. It's been going on for a week, already. I suppose I was plum blind to any of that vulgar advertising that made you so ill, Sugar. You know, you really need a comm if you want to meet men. One needs a communication device before one can ping you, eh? So, until you can save enough to get yourself a little comm, we need to go out and find men in person. That's why I came over, Honey... I cannot exactly ping you if you do not have a comm, can I?"

Sarah threw up her arms and said, "I am actually saving to buy a new one, but I just spent all my money decorating my new place, here." Sarah sighed, "You should have given me advance warning, Georgia. You know I hate spontaneous things like this. I like my little world carefully planned out. Prepared."

"Well," Georgia opened a compact and checked her lipstick, "I would have called, but... well, we already established getting hold of you is a challenge, Sugar. So here I am in person...want my autograph?"

She smiled and popped her mirror back into her bag, striking an exaggerated glamour pose for a moment.

Sarah replied gently pleading, "I'm

about to make myself dinner," Sarah protested as she walked to the kitchen and indicated the frozen chicken in her kitchen sink. Sarah opened up her freezer door, pulled out a tub of ice, and poured it over the chicken.

Georgia looked confused.

Sarah said, "I don't have room in my fridge to defrost it properly and you know I'd never defrost frozen chicken at room temperature. The ice is a compromise."

"Compromise?" Georgia teased as she started to plump a decorative throw pillow. She added, "You mean like how you compromise on men?"

"Not fair, Georgia," Sarah replied. "I'm just picky about what man I want to get to know."

Georgia stood up walked toward the door, rolling her eyes as she tossed the pillow back into its place on the sofa.

"I've already heard your story of that Daily Memo reporter who whisked you away on horseback to...." Georgia paused for dramatic effect, "...to host a field trip with kids at Library." She sighed with a flourish and added with sarcasm, "Will your romances never cease?"

Sarah protested, "Bjorn Esterday is a good reporter and the Daily Memo is the most accurate newspaper of any in corporate city."

"Most accurate?" Georgia scoffed, "They didn't even report the full story about how the Twins took power in AromaX. Now that was a corporate city which once was a welcoming destination, but now ...yuck."

"What do you mean?"

Georgia whispered as if she was repeating gossip in a crowded room, "I heard people died."

"Are you listening to conspiracy

theories?" Sarah shook her head, "I recall when power suddenly shifted away from a particular family and abruptly fell into the Twins clutches. The people of AromaX asked the Board of Directors to vote and... they voted for the Twins. The end."

"Well," Georgia lowered her voice to a whisper, "What your Daily Memo newspaper left out was that the day before the vote, four key members of the board had accidents. One ate something with seafood and the anaphylactic shock killed him in the Emergency Room. Another accidentally crashed a crop duster down into one of the flower fields and died on impact. Another had a fatal heart attack...and the last one slipped and fell in the bath and accidentally drowned in ten inches of water."

"Oh... Hmm... They still could all be unfortunate.... accidents..." Sarah sympathized, "But not a conspiracy."

"No?" Georgia said, "AromaX City stopped being a place where the people voted on issues. Most votes won. Once the Twins encouraged their people to keep protesting the winner if it wasn't them... you know... eventually bickering started, trust eroded, Twins moved in, said only they could fix things, but did not fix anything...and voting stopped."

"Stopped?" Sarah asked, "But there was a ruling family so there is no need for elections and dragging the people out to vote..."

Georgia shook her head, "The Twins said they knew best for the people, but they were not benevolent dictators. They just wanted the money allocated to the people for themselves. The Twins said they knew what was best, but they took everything for themselves and then blamed the pople for the bad situation."

"I heard the ruling family was tired of ruling in AromaX." Sarah casually mentioned, 'They invited the Twins in."

"That's what your Daily Memo says, but I have a friend."

"A friend or boyfriend?" Sarah quipped.

"Does it matter, Sugar?" Georgia retorted, "Point is, the ruling family did some research and found the most prosperous cities included the people in making decisions. Voting. Elections. All that. I mean your own Courtly City gained power when gasoline powered vehicles ran out of gasoline and Courtly ruling family harnessed solar and hydrogen and compressed air as power sources for buildings and wheeled-vehicles."

Sarah added, "Right, Courtly used to be a bankrupted town which was purchased at auction, and original Mr. Courtly spent money on fuel research and deployed it in the city. Drive on a special road and your vehicle recharges...stuff like that other cities did not have. So people came here. We have a lot of resources other cities do not have....but we also do not really vote on things."

"According to my friend, the ruling family thought if the citizens of AromaX had a voice in how the city was run, they would be more engaged in their jobs and protective of the city. But, then the Twins came to town promising more profits for everyone and better services if the citizens abolished public voting and put them in charge...it was a lie, but now it is the way it is and no going back."

"Well, no corporate city allows public voting," Sarah agreed. "Maybe you should date more locally, Georgia. AromaX is a long way away from here."

"Some cities did let the people vote on how things were managed," Georgia wagged a finger as she continued, "But the Twins said it would be easier for the people to let the Twins make all the decisions. They ran what they called a campaign."

"Campaign? Never heard of it. Do you mean champagne?"

Georgia shrugged, "Yeah? Campaign

was like non-stop promises, an absolute fairy tale..." Georgia mocked while mimicking some slogans, "Schools will be better if the Twins run AromaX. You'll get richer if the Twins run AromaX. We'll have more products to export if the Twins run AromaX. You'll get more respect if the Twins run AromaX. AromaX might get attacked and we don't have a strong soldier police force, so the Twins will protect AromaX..."

Georgia paused for a moment, then shrugged. "So, the people of AromaX gave it a try and agreed to have a committee on the Board of Directors vote on behalf of the citizens."

"Why not? Why not give the Twins a try?"

"Why not? Because sometimes there is no going back."

"What did your friend say happened with the committee of directors to vote on behalf of the AroaX citizens?"

Georgia explained, "The members of the committee needed to replace the four board members who had suddenly died. Those four alternates voted for the dictatorship of the Twins. It was a 'coup' where the Twins quietly took over the Board of Directors, which means they took over AromaX. But your Daily Memo doesn't tell you any of that."

"I think," Sarah smiled patiently, "That's because that sort of story is something you'd read about in some conspiracy-riddled cotton-candy rag... not a real newspaper like Daily Memo."

Georgia flashed a huge smile, "You're right, Sugar. I can't really believe my source of that AromaX story, can I? I should be more productive with my time. Off to man-hunting we go!"

"But," Sarah shook her head trying to come up with an excuse as she lingered to straighten a picture of brightly colored red and pink flowers painted in the manner of the old Dutch masters.

Georgia grabbed Sarah's wrist, leading her toward the door. "I'm just glad I caught you before you changed into something calico, patch-worked, or flannel," Georgia grinned. "Sarah, you can cook that thawing chicken when we get back."

Succumbing to the pressure of her new coworker and friend, Sarah sighed, "Oh, all right." She gave in and followed Georgia Peach out the door.

"Besides," Georgia added as she scooped up Sarah's handbag and shoved it at her, "Maybe we will both meet a reporter tonight. The Daily Memo Newspaper employs quite a few. You never know..."

"Doubt there are others like Bjorn Esterday," Sarah sighed softly to herself.

"Oh, right," Georgia giggled, "the guy you met once. Once. Come on, Sarah. If Bjorn Esterday hasn't tracked you down by now... I mean... Well, I'm not trying to be mean, Sugar... but goodness!"

Sarah, crestfallen, said, "I just thought he... and I... we...connected..."

Georgia, now sorry she had been so callously playful at the expense of Sarah's heart, softly replied, "All I'm saying is.... where is this Bjorn Esterday? Maybe he moved away...Some loves cannot survive geographic distance. Except in fairy tales, that is. In real life, men are too lazy to cross the miles to try and find you. Honeybunch, I'm sure you did connect with that Bjorn guy. He's probably... just... well... someplace else. That's why we both need to find somebody new. And make it prompt."

Georgia scooted out as the door closed behind them. Sarah held up her handbag and waited for the sound of her door to click shut, indicating it was locked. She opened her bag and the soft interior light illuminated the contents inside. She found her train transportation pass and closed her bag, shutting off all internal purse light.

Then, Sarah and Georgia headed out.

Georgia chirped, "Off to the Courtly train station to get to the Watson conference, then clubbing…"

Sarah Paradise's thoughts drifted to Bjorn Esterday. Neither Sarah nor Georgia realized that far away Bjorn Esterday, Reporter at the Daily Memo, was in a predicament he might not survive.

5 What Just Happened?

We step back a month earlier to see what Lou Pole Linden and Otto Mattick discussed in the lab. We see that Linden lacks respect for the former ruling family member.

Otto expresses his frustrations to his nephew, Topliner, back at their humble apartment.

This abode is a stark contrast to the lavish dwelling they used to live in when the Mattick name was the ruling family of AromaX before the Twins came to power and forcibly seized the city of AromaX.

Meanwhile, thousands of miles away, we see Longfellow and Warren Piece, former residents of AromaX, now living in a remote location. Here they tend to a winery in Maastricht and also welcome other AromaX refugees who wish to escape to oppression of the Twin's authoritarian leadership in AromaX.

Back in Courtly City, Sarah Paradise, school teacher, and her colleague and fellow teacher, Georgia Peach, head to the train station for an evening out. Georgia is trying to get Sarah to find a new man and stop thinking about that Bjorn Esterday who just vanished.

But, mystery awaits...

6 Did You Know...

In Chapter 3 (continuous chapter 6) Longfellow ponders his love of plants. Plants can be used for food, for fragrance, and much more.

Did you know some plants can consume chemicals, such as formaldehyde or ammonia, which are harmful to humans?

Those plants are great to have indoors, but be aware, they can be toxic to dogs and cats. Pet owners should take precautions to keep such plants out of reach of pets. Always evaluate the toxic level of plants before bringing any plant inside your home.

The following chemicals can evidence specific symptoms in humans.

1. **Formaldehyde**. This is found in paper bags, paper towels, and even facial tissue. It is also contained in some synthetic fabrics, plywood, and more. Toxic levels may appear in humans after a brief duration of exposure. Contact a doctor if you experience: Irritation to eyes, nose, mouth, and throat. Medical examination may also reveal swelling of the larynx and lungs.

2. **Benzene**. This is found in resins, synthetic fibers, dyes, plastics, detergents, and some drugs and pesticides. Benzene is commonly found in vehicle exhaust, tobacco smoke, glue, paint and even furniture wax. If you suspect you have been exposed and also experience symptoms, contact a doctor. After exposure, you may also have increased heart rate, eye stress,. headaches, drowsiness, confusion, or if you have fainted.

3. **Xylene**. This is found in leather, paint, and nail polish as well as hair dyes. It is also found in some printed goods. Xylene, like Benzene, is found in tobacco smoke and vehicle exhaust. If you have been exposed, you may want to contact a doctor if you experience confusion, headaches, dizziness, or throat and mouth irritation. A doctor may diagnose that exposure to Xylene resulted in heart problems, coma, as well as kidney and liver damage.

4. **Ammonia**. This is found in window cleaners and floor waxes. Gardeners may discover ammonia in fertilizers. Ammonia has been used in the past as "smelling salts" to revive people who faint. If you have been over exposed to Ammonia and experience eye irritation, coughing, and sore throat, consult a doctor.

5. **Trichloroethylene**. This is found in paints, printing inks, lacquers, varnishes, adhesives, paint remover, typewriter

correction fluids and cleaning fluids. It is used with other chemicals as a refrigerant, as well as a solvent for grease, oil, wax, and tars. Even short term exposure could result in dizziness, headache, excitement, nausea and vomiting followed by drowsiness and coma. See a doctor.

NASA (National Aeronautics and Space Administration) generated a report (INTERIOR LANDSCAPE PLANTS FOR INDOOR AIR POLLUTION ABATEMENT FINAL REPORT-- SEPTEMBER 15, 1989) to find out which houseplants consume these toxins to contribute to fostering cleaner indoor air along with a carbon air filter.

This work was jointly supported by the NASA Office of Commercial Programs-- Technology Utilization Division, and the Associated Landscape Contractors of America (**ALCA**).

Many plants are attractive, but the following lists plants which consumed at least four of the toxins discussed earlier. That means the listed plants with a carbon air filter, created air with better breathing quality.

1. English Ivy (*Hedera helix*)

2. Verigated Snake Plant or Mother-in-Law's Tongue (*Sansevieria trifasciata Laurentii*)

3. Red-Edged Dracaena or Marginata (*Dracaena marginata*)

4. Peace Lily (*Spathiphyllum 'Mauna Loa'*)

5. Florist's Chrysanthemum or Pot mum (*Chrysanthemum morifolium*)

Houseplants coupled with activated carbon filters together can improve indoor air quality. This study was created to alleviate "sick building syndrome".

Did you know that SBS, or Sick Building Syndrome is used to describe when a person's ill feelings seem to be associated with time spent in a particular building. It can also be Closed-building-syndrom. Generally, the chemicals are found in paint, adhesives, carpeting, cleaning agents, and upholstered furniture. These chemicals can emit volatile organic compounds (VOCs). contaminants from outside of the building can include exhaust from motor vehicles and other industrial plants in the area.

Frequently, the ailment cause cannot be identified by traditional methods.

Sometimes, the building can appear to cause chronic disease because the individual is living or working regularly in that building.

Risk-factors include:
- ✓ Industrial-environments or industrial-exposures or poor ventilation-systems
- ✓ Air-contamination or poor air-quality
- ✓ Indoor-air-pollution and poor indoor environment quality;
- ✓ Enclosed workplace, which may put office workers at risk
- ✓ Respiratory-system-disorders such as bronchial-asthma or Respiratory-hypersensitivity; Epidemiology

<u>Symptoms of SBS could include</u>:
- ✓ Chronic nasal irritation
- ✓ Headaches or dizziness
- ✓ Skin rashes,
- ✓ Itchy eyes and mucous membrane irritation of eyes, nose, and throat;
- ✓ Vague issues such as fatigue. Do note that fatigue can be caused by other things besides chemicals. Here are some reasons for feeling tired.
  - ■ Sleep apnea, where you suddenly stop breathing at night.
  - ■ Not getting enough sleep
  - ■ Sensitivity to odors
  - ■ General aches and pains.
  - ■ Eating high sugar, high carbohydrate diet where your blood-sugar levels spike and fall.
  - ■ Not eating at all
  - ■ Not drinking enough water
  - ■ Anemia where your blood does not have enough iron. Low levels of iron means your body does not get the oxygen it needs.
  - ■ Depression
  - ■ Dehydration, or not drinking enough water
  - ■ Changing times you work or travel

which forces you to adjust to new time zones. Try to maintain a regular bed time and wake-up time even when you are not working or in school.

■ Too much caffeine. If you were used to a lot of coffee, cola or teas with caffeine and then stop, you may experience symptoms of withdrawal, including headaches or feeling tired. Instead slowly start drinking more water and fewer caffeine-filled beverages.

■ Ask your doctor if your fatigue could be related to
  ✧ food allergies,
  ✧ Chronic fatigue syndrome (CFS) and Fibromyalgia,
  ✧ Heart Disease,
  ✧ Diabetes,
  ✧ UTI. Urinary tract infections (UTIs) include pain or burning during urination, or the feeling that you need to urinate urgently or frequently. But UTIs can also cause fatigue and weakness. Some treatments for UTI includes antibiotics.

✧ Also ask your doctor about Hypothyroidism--The thyroid is a gland that regulates the metabolism, or how fast the body converts fuel into energy. Slow working thyroids may cause depression, fatigue and even weight gain. Ask your doctor about your hormone levels.

It can also include any of the symptoms mentioned earlier when describing specific chemicals.

7 Vocabulary

This fictional series introduces some words unique to this world. Also used are standard terms which we encourage you to investigate in a dictionary for your own edification. A consolidated full list of vocabulary for all GONE books is located in the Conversation Station supplemental book.

Gloated. This has been used since the mid 1500s to refer to an attentive scornful gaze. A modern definition would be to look at something with smug satisfaction.

Cassock. Since the1540s, this term meant a "long loose gown or outer cloak."

Botanicals. this is a term meaning something which is related to plants. It could be a drug substance made from part of a plant, as from roots, leaves, bark, or berries. In the 1650s, it meant "concerned with the study or cultivation of plants,"

Botticelli. Is the surname of Italian artist Sandro Botticelli who painted in the 1400s in Florence, Italy. He made many famous paintings, including one "Birth of Venus" (1483-1485) which shows a fully grown goddess named Venus arriving on the waves to shore in an open sea shell to celebrate her birth.

Demeaned. Caused severe loss of dignity or respect for someone or something else. In use since the 1600's.

Vigorously. Done in a way that involves physical strength or effort. In use since the 1300's. Thought to come from medieval Latin, *vigere*, meaning "to be lively, flourish, thrive".

Cherish. Used since early 14th century. Protect and care for someone lovingly.

ACA: Anti-Corporate Activity. The ACA is sounded publicly by the SPs when their sensors pick up the presence of the AnCors. When an ACA alert is in progress, no wheeled vehicles are permitted on the pathways. This is to allow the SPs on horseback to chase the offender. For the citizens, the only mode of transportation available to them during an ACA is anything without a wheel-on-the-streets. This includes trains, horses, or any other mode of transportation not on the street. Since the AnCors use older gasoline-powered cars and trucks, the SPs know that if those are on the road, then there are probably AnCors operating those vehicles. They become an easy target for the SPs/

AnCor: Anti-Corporatists. This group has many chapters, but the one located in Courtly City at the time of this writing is Percy Snatcher, who relies on his subordinate, Slash. The group started as a protest to the increasing power of corporations, but bit by bit, the members were cut off from societies resources by the very corporations they tried to fight. As a result, those who are a member of the AnCors at the time of this writing live "off the grid" of the corporate kingdom. They use older technologies of the past, abandoned by the citizens of the corporate city. They also have learned to survive by selling their mercenary talents to the highest bidder, which, hypocritically, embodies the very spirit of "anything for a profit" which they claim they are trying to combat in formal corporations. Ironically, some citizens who are opposed to the indiscriminate power of the corporation quietly live in the society with professions such as investigative reporter or school teacher. They are in a position to really make a change for the better, but they do it by solving mysteries and exposing the truth, not by threatening innocent lives for a price, as the AnCors of Courtly City do.

Earthie: This is a derogatory term used to refer to a member of the Earth Farmer Community. The Earth Farmers are a group of people who eschew the technology of the modern world in Courtly City and instead quietly and peacefully live and hone farming and other hand-craft skills, including but not limited to quilting. They are considered a Christian religious community.

Earthshake: An archaic translation would be earthquake. This is a term referring to the shaking of the ground and at times, to the point of opening a fissure

SP: Soldier Police, the enforcement body assigned to each corporate kingdom, such as Courtly City.

ABOUT Wynter Sommers

Wynter Sommers is the pseudonym for an American writing team, which harnesses multiple skills in technology, research, history and education. Formally trained with a PhD in Education, Wynter Sommers blends academic classroom experience, with corporate sophistication, and a passion for developing more effective student insights through engaging storytelling.

Wynter Sommers has a heart to inspire creativity and develop critical thinking skills, all to encourage readers to make wise choices in life.

Wynter Sommers takes each story and weaves the plot with classic gripping elements, which endure throughout repeated readings, revealing new meanings each time the story is explored. The small choices a reader makes in real life could have a lasting effect in future generations. This set of stories shows the origin of not just Bjorn Esterday and Sarah Paradise, but of their ancestors and the sort of world which was established, which unfolded in each generation until Bjorn and Sarah met.

It is rewarding to learn of heartfelt, thought provoking conversations taking place globally about the characters of these books. Should the reader be presented with extraordinary circumstances, it is the sincerest wish that they act with honor, truth and integrity to overcome obstacles in real life whilst the reader hones skills of self-reliance and collaborative teamwork despite barriers outside of the reader's control. Wynter Sommers hopes you enjoy the other **Bjorn Esterday Was not Born Yesterday** stories in this series.